THE ARCTIC CHALLENGE

THE ARCTIC CHALLENGE

BEAR GRYLLS
ILLUSTRATED BY EMMA McCANN

This edition published in Great Britain in 2019 by

4th Floor, Victoria House, Bloomsbury Square
London WC1B 4DA

A CIP catalogue record for this book
is available from the British Library.

ISBN: 978–1–786–96079–5
Also available as an ebook and in audio

9

Typeset in OpenDyslexia
Printed and bound in Great Britain
by Clays Ltd, Elcograf S.p.A.

Bear Grylls is an imprint of Bonnier Books UK,
owned by Bonnier Books
Sveavägen 56, Stockholm, Sweden

www.bonnierbooks.co.uk

To the young survivor
reading this book for the first time.
May your eyes always be wide open
to adventure, and your heart full
of courage and determination to
see your dreams through.

1

LEFT AND WRITE

Joe laughed, excited and dizzy,
as the world spun round and
round. It was just like being
inside a washing machine.

He was strapped inside a huge
transparent plastic bubble, with
his friend Omar, bouncing around
a sandy track. This was the Bubble
Run, one of Camp's many activities.

Joe could see the other bubble trundling behind them, with Lily and Mia in it.

"Bend coming!" Omar called.

"I see it," Joe said confidently.

To steer the bubble, they both had to lean in the same direction at the same time.

"And ... lean!" said Omar.

The bubble rolled around the bend, but they were going a bit too fast and it overshot, straight into a tree.

They bounced off and Omar and Joe laughed. This was fun! But Omar spotted a problem.

"Hey, we're going to
hit the girls! Lean left!"

Deliberate bubble bumping
wasn't allowed. It spoiled the
fun for everyone. Joe leaned.

"No, *left!*"

Joe quickly leaned the other
way. Too late. The bubbles
bounced off each other.

"We've got to get out of their way," said Omar. "Lean right."

Joe felt his brain jam up. Right, left, which was which?

"Right!" Omar urged. "Come on, Joe, or we'll hit them again!"

The girls' bubble thumped into theirs again. Omar saw where they were rolling in alarm.

"We're right at the top of the slope! Lean left ..."

Joe panicked. It was too late. The two bubbles were out of control.

For a few dizzying seconds,

the whole world whirled as they bounced down the slope. The bubbles stopped at the bottom with one last bump.

With their heads still spinning, they unstrapped themselves and clambered out.

Everyone was dizzy and a bit dazed, but Joe was relieved to see that no one looked hurt. Well, almost. Lily looked slightly more confused than the others.

Joe was going to say something but then a leader came running down, a look of worry all over her face. She asked if everyone was okay, and Joe had to admit that it was his fault.

"Omar was telling me to go right but ... uh ... I just get muddled ..."

Joe expected everyone to laugh, but no one did. The leader just gave a sympathetic smile. She pointed out that Joe and Omar both wore watches on their left wrists – so from now on, Omar should tell Joe 'watch' and 'not-watch' instead of 'left' and 'right'.

They pushed their bubbles back to the top, and finished the Bubble Run without bumping out of control again.

But the fun had gone out of it for Joe. He just felt stupid.

Afterwards, they were all at lunch with the rest of Camp in the meal clearing. They picked a table in the

7

shade of a tree. Joe let the others
chat while he studied his hands.
He *had* to get this right.

Once, for one day only, Joe had
tried marking his hands, 'L' and 'R'.
Then someone noticed the 'L' and
asked what it was for. He had made
up some excuse, and gone straight off
to the bathroom to wash the letters
away. It was just embarrassing.

'Watch' or 'not-watch' should work.
As long as he always wore a watch,
and remembered which wrist to put
it on.

But, apart from Omar, people would just keep on saying 'left' and 'right'.

Once, Joe had had an easy way of remembering directions.

Left was the way you turned out of his house to head for town.

Right was the other way.

This had worked for him, until a teacher at school had tried to be helpful.

"Your *right* hand is the hand you *write* with, Joe!" she had said with a smile.

She hadn't noticed Joe was left-handed.

So now his thoughts went
something like this.

Left is *town direction* which
is *this* way but that's my writing
hand and I *write* with my *right*
except I don't I write with my
left and ... AARGH!

That was when his brain sort
of locked up. There was just too
much thinking going on up there.

And that was how it had been
for him ever since.

"Hey, Joe." Lily interrupted his
thoughts. "Maybe you'd like this?"

She pushed a compass across
the table at him.

Joe wondered if she was trying
to be helpful, or if she just thought
she was being funny.

"Why do you think I need a
compass?" he demanded. "'Cos
I get lost so easily?"

"No, it's not that," she said.
"Really. Just consider it a gift."

Joe could see Lily was serious. She really was giving him a present.

"Okay. Uh ... thanks?" Joe put the compass in his pocket. Maybe it would come in handy.

Meanwhile, Mia was still making out that basically the crash hadn't been her fault even though it had turned out she'd not bothered to strap in properly.

Joe fought back a sudden wave of irritation.

He wanted to yell, "It wasn't all our fault!" But anything he said might just remind people that he couldn't tell left and right.

Abruptly, Joe stood up. Omar looked up in surprise.

"Hey, Joe, you haven't eaten."

"That's okay. You have it," Joe said. "I just need to ... go somewhere."

Omar looked anxious.

"You sure you'll be okay?"

Joe realised his friend was looking out for him. Omar was worried Joe would get lost.

"I'll be fine," he said, turning away. "I've got a compass."

2

NO DIRECTION HOME

Joe slouched through the trees, kicking at the leaves, feeling grumpy.

"Stupid, stupid, stupid," he muttered.

But he knew he wasn't stupid. Not really.

Joe had a friend at school with reading challenges. His friend wasn't stupid either. Some kids found maths hard. Some kids couldn't play a musical instrument. Joe got confused about directions. It didn't make any of them stupid.

The only person telling Joe that he was stupid was Joe himself.

But it was just so annoying!

And he was hungry. Joe's stomach rumbled, loud enough for anyone else to hear. If there had been anyone around. There wasn't, because Joe had wandered deep into the woods. He couldn't hear any of the sounds of Camp.

Joe sighed. It was stupid to
be hungry when you didn't need
to be. He should make his way
back. Maybe he could get there
before the end of lunch.

Joe turned around – and stopped.

Which way?

Joe set off through the gap between
two trees. He had come this way ...

Hadn't he?

Or maybe he had come from
over there, past that bush?

Joe rolled his eyes. Yup, he
had managed to get lost again.

Normally, Joe made sure he went
everywhere with his friends. They
all just stuck together and he didn't
have to think about directions.

He'd managed to get himself lost at
Camp once before, and accidentally
won a game of Capture the Flag. But
nothing good was going to happen
accidentally now, he thought glumly.

Then Joe remembered the compass.
He pulled it out and studied the dial.
Four directions, one needle, always
pointing north. Easy. He just had to
follow the needle...

But which direction?

Joe groaned out loud. He had no idea where the Camp clearing was. So, he had no idea which direction to follow.

And he was still hungry.

"Well, that was clever, wasn't it?" he muttered.

Joe put his hands on his head, and thought.

There were paths and tracks running through the woods. There were lots of clearings. And there was a fence around Camp.

So, if he just picked a direction and kept going, then sooner or later he would find *something*. Maybe another kid. Maybe the fence. If he found the fence, then he could just follow that and he would find the main gate.

Joe picked a direction and started walking with a determined stride.

But after a while he had to walk around some bushes and then he couldn't see where he had come from.

Joe carried on, a bit more hesitantly.

Then he had to take a detour to cross a stream.

Now which way had he been going?

Joe felt his heart and breathing start to speed up. What if he just went round and round in circles in the woods forever?

The compass could help him head in a straight line!

Joe shot another look at the dial.

"Oh, what?"

So much for that idea. The needle was just going round and round. And instead of four directions on the compass, there were five.

"Fine, great, whatever," Joe muttered through his teeth. He stuffed the compass back into his pocket.

"So, next idea?"

Joe stared at the nearest tree, like it might make a helpful suggestion. Once, he'd heard someone on TV saying that trees could help you tell your direction.

But he couldn't remember how.

Joe turned a slow circle and tried to remember what it was about trees and directions. It just wasn't coming to him.

"Stupid trees," Joe groaned.

He stopped moving, but now he was dizzy and it felt like everything was spinning around him.

"*Aargh!*" Joe shouted in frustration.

He stumbled, and suddenly realised that it didn't just feel like the trees were spinning. They really *were* spinning. Round and round and round.

The ground underneath him was shifting and spinning. Joe dropped dizzily to his knees, before he fell over.

A freezing wind blasted its way through the wood. Joe yelped and clutched his arms. He was only wearing a T-shirt, and his bare skin had turned rough with goose pimples.

Joe shivered and his teeth chattered.

He realised he wasn't kneeling on earth and leaves.

He was kneeling on ... ice?

Joe looked up.

He was on a slab of floating ice, in the middle of a river. Other lumps of ice jostled and bumped each other as they slowly drifted downstream.

The river was wide and swollen.
Trees on either side looked like
Christmas trees, covered with
snow.

The slab wobbled under Joe.
It was longer than a grown-up's
height, but it was only as wide
as his outstretched arms.

There was no sign of Camp, or the woods that Joe had just been walking in. And his shivers were getting uncontrollable. If something didn't happen soon, he might just shiver to death.

"Hello," came a voice nearby. "Over here!"

Joe's head whipped round. A man was running along the snow-covered bank.

3

GO WITH THE FLOE

The man was dressed in warm, padded clothes, with a fur-lined hood. He wasn't far from Joe either, near enough that he didn't have to shout.

At least, he wouldn't have had to shout if there wasn't an ice-packed river flowing between them.

The man stopped by a small tree.

A blade flashed in his hand as he hacked at a slim branch.

"You can't swim in water this cold," he called. "You'll have to push yourself over to the bank. Take this."

The man jogged along until he was level with Joe, then threw the branch like a javelin. It hit the ice just in front of Joe.

Joe's numb fingers struggled to hold onto it. He tried to stand up. The ice wobbled again and he quickly dropped back to his knees.

"Don't stand," the man called. "Stay just as you are. You need to keep your centre of gravity low. Just push gently. Make sure not to push yourself off the ice."

Joe nervously put the branch into the water. The ice started to tilt, but he felt the end of the branch touch the bottom. He put all his strength into his arms.

The ice moved, the end of the branch stayed where it was, but soon Joe was leaning right out and the ice was tilting. He quickly pulled the branch back in. The ice splashed back to being level again.

Bit by bit, Joe pushed his piece of ice towards the bank. The movement warmed him up – a little. His teeth didn't chatter so much and his shivering had slowed down. But he still couldn't feel his hands.

"You're doing really well!"

Joe didn't dare look up, but it was good to know the man was still there, encouraging him.

At last the ice bumped against the bank. The man was right there. He held his arm out.

"And, jump!"

The ice started to rock again as Joe stood up, and he jumped without any delay. The ice shot away backwards, but the man grabbed Joe and swung him to dry land.

"Brilliant!" he said, smiling. "You handled that so well. Now let's get you warm!" He pointed to a clump of trees nearby. "My camp's back here."

Joe's arms and feet were going numb as they hurried through the pine trees to a clearing. There, Joe saw the most beautiful sight of his life. A small fire, crackling away, with a steaming metal pot hanging over it.

Joe crouched next to the fire while the man pulled things out of his rucksack.

A warm, padded coat and a pair of
thick trousers. A thermal hat. Gloves.
Thick socks. Fur-lined boots.

Joe tried to pull everything on
over the clothes he was already
wearing. His fingers were so numb
he couldn't get a grip.

"Here, let me help." The man
held the coat while Joe slipped
his arms into the sleeves. "Every
second counts when you're fighting
hypothermia."

"Wh-what's that?" Joe stammered
through chattering teeth.

The man helped Joe do up the coat.

"It's when your body core gets so cold, it can't warm itself up again. Don't worry, you'll be okay. We acted quickly."

The man set the hat on Joe's head.

"It looks like I'm your guide out of here," he said cheerfully. "My name's Bear. Are you ready for some real adventure?"

"I g-guess s-so."

Joe's teeth still chattered. He pulled the hood up. Now he was thoroughly wrapped in warm clothing. He wasn't getting colder, but there was still a chill deep inside him.

"Thanks. I'm J-Joe. And I'm still c-cold."

"Let's run on the spot," Bear suggested. He demonstrated, and Joe ran with him. He felt a very faint flicker of warmth deep down inside his body.

"And do this." Bear started to wheel his arms around like a windmill. "It looks a bit odd, but it's a great way to drive the blood back into your limbs."

Joe swung his arms like Bear had shown him, for about a minute. His fingers started to tingle with pins and needles, but soon he was feeling almost back to normal.

Meanwhile, Bear poured him a drink from the pot over the fire.

"Fancy a cup of hot pine-needle tea?" he asked. "It's full of energy and vitamins. It's just what you need!"

"Thank you."

Joe took it gratefully. He didn't
care what kind of tea it was, as long
as it was warm. The heat from the
cup soaked in through his gloves
and warmed his hands.

They sat on logs either side of
the fire, and Bear poured a cup for
himself. Joe sipped at his tea and felt
the glow inside him growing stronger.

"Thank you for helping me," Joe
said. "But, um, where are we, exactly?
I was trying to follow a compass but
I think I've got really lost."

"Compasses won't work up here
in the Arctic," Bear agreed. "They
point to the magnetic north pole,

but we're so far north we're almost on top of the magnetic pole anyway. A compass would just go in circles."

Bear sipped at his tea. "I was trekking to the coast when an ice dam broke and the river flooded. It blocked my path. Having to find another route has added a good twenty-four hours to my journey."

"Couldn't you get across it?" Joe asked.

Bear smiled as he shook his head.

"You've got the survival spirit, Joe! It's always important to explore your options. Water's really powerful, even when it's slow. A river like that one, flowing at seven miles per hour, could wash a house away, so I wasn't going to try it. And the cold would be too much," Bear explained.

"I'm heading for an abandoned hunting lodge to spend the night in," Bear went on. "It's by a lake, a few hours walk from here."

"It's lucky for me you were here, then," Joe said thoughtfully.

Bear smiled.

"Well, that's true! Good things often happen when we least expect them to. I'd only stopped for a rest and a hot drink, but it was the right time and the right place to meet you."

Bear and Joe both took another sip
of tea. Joe felt the warmth inside him.

Bear smiled and said, "We'll be
doing this a lot. We need to be
hydrated and warm, and daytime
temperatures here can be down
to minus twenty. I've got some
provisions – but, of course, I only
brought enough for one person and
for a shorter trek!"

Bear saw Joe's expression and said,
"Don't worry. We can forage off the
land. Survival is about finding ways
of using nature, not fighting it. But
I should warn you ..."

"It's going to be tough, isn't it?"
said Joe.

Bear nodded.

"That's right. But we have the right gear, we know where we're going and we've got a positive attitude. Most of all, we've got each other – a team. Everything a survivor needs."

Joe could feel himself relax. Bear obviously believed they could do this, and that meant Joe began to believe it too.

Until a thought struck him.

He had *really* better avoid getting lost in these woods ...

4

SNOW RIPPLES

As he helped Bear get ready for
the trek, there was one question
burning inside Joe.

They kicked snow over the fire,
and Bear gave Joe an extendable
walking stick. Joe adjusted it to his
own height while Bear cut himself
a fresh stick from a branch.

Bear also passed Joe a one-litre water bottle to pack with snow while Bear finished working on his stick.

"That's great," Bear said when Joe had finished. "Put it in your coat's inside pocket, and your body heat will melt the snow into fresh water. We'll head due east and walk until the day warms up and the snow melts in the bottles. Are you ready?"

Joe nodded. He tried not to look nervous.

But as soon as they started walking, the question he'd been holding inside came bursting out.

"Bear, how will we know where to go? Which way is due east?"

"That's a great question. There are clues all around if we know where to look," Bear said. "For a start, we're following the way the wind usually blows – that's called the prevailing wind."

"But sometimes the wind changes direction," Joe pointed out.

"You're right, but 'prevailing' means that it *mostly* comes from one direction, just not always. Here, it mostly blows towards the coast, which is east. That's why this bush is thicker on one side than the other, because it grows better away from the wind. Another sign is the moss growing on the trees."

Bear tapped a trunk with his stick.

"Do you see how it's only growing on this side? It's the side that the sun doesn't reach. In other words, the north side. With a bit of practice, you'll soon be able to work out the general direction."

"So, *that's* the thing with trees!" Joe said. He was determined to learn.

They kept going. Joe was still happy to let Bear set the direction, but he kept an eye out for clues that they were still heading east.

A couple of times his feet caught on tree roots and other things hidden beneath the snow and he stumbled. Bear showed him how to prod the ground with his stick before each step, to check.

Soon they came to the end of the trees. Joe stared. Ahead of them was a wide open plain of snow, smooth and white. There was the occasional bush sticking up, and the odd tree. But Joe didn't think even Bear would be able to tell the wind direction from those. It was a lot of space to get lost in.

Bear seemed to know what Joe was thinking. He pointed at some mountains on the horizon.

"We'll be okay, Joe. Those mountains will make excellent landmarks. As long as we head for that big one, over there, we'll be going the right way."

"But supposing those clouds cover the mountains up?" Joe asked cautiously. He was so used to getting lost that he could generally see the flaw in any clever plan to stay on track.

"That's another good question."
Bear pointed his stick down at the
ground. "Look closely. Can you see
that the surface of the snow is
rippled?"

Joe peered at the ground. He had
never noticed it before, because the
ripples were only a few millimetres
high. And they were almost the
same white as the rest of the snow.
But they were there, about ten
centimetres apart.

They disappeared off into the
distance, always pointing in the
same direction.

"That's the prevailing wind again," Bear said. "These are called *sastrugi*, and the wind blows them all the same way. So, again, we have something to work out our own direction from."

Joe still kept one eye on the ground as he followed Bear across the snow, just in case the sastrugi all decided to wiggle round and face another way.

They reminded him of the contour lines on maps, but that wasn't much comfort. Joe had never really got on well with maps.

The snow on the plain was deeper and thicker than in the woods. Joe followed Bear's example of lifting each foot well out of the snow before he put it down again. It felt weird,

and it made his thighs ache. But it
was less tiring than dragging his legs
through the snow without lifting them.

After a while they approached
a scraggly bush that was sticking
up from the snow. It didn't look like
much to Joe – just some bare stalks
and a few withered leaves. But Bear
knelt by it and poked some of the
leaves apart.

Joe crouched beside him and saw some small blue berries nestled together.

"Perfect. These are crowberries," Bear said. "In this cold we need twice the normal amount of calories to keep going. These will top us up and give us a little bit of vitamin C besides."

Bear started to pluck some. Joe spotted a cluster of dark spots in the snow by his knee. Some of the berries must have dropped off already, he thought. Joe fumbled to pick them up with his gloved hands.

Hmm. He held them up to his face, to study. They didn't look exactly like berries. More sort of leathery.

"And those would be reindeer droppings," Bear said with a smile.

"Yuck!" Joe quickly flung them away.

"It looks like the reindeer are going the same way we are," said Bear quietly. "See the tracks?"

The prints that trailed through the snow were shaped like two apple pips, side by side – but much bigger. If Joe spread all his fingers out on one hand, he could just about cover an entire print.

"They're big!"

"Yup. They spread the pressure as they walk on snow, to stop them sinking in," Bear said. "Now ..."

The prints disappeared over a small rise, in the direction Joe and Bear had been heading.

"We'll go carefully," Bear murmured. "I don't want to have to go out of our way to avoid them but reindeer have excellent vision and are easily spooked. Plus, they can run ten times faster than a human, so there's not much chance if they decide you're a threat and charge you."

Joe and Bear crept forward and peeked over the edge of the rise.

There were the reindeer. A herd of about ten or twelve, the size of small horses, with reddish-brown fur. Some of them had massive, lethal-looking antlers sprouting from their heads.

Joe was happy keeping a distance. He didn't want those heading for him, especially not if they were going to be travelling ten times faster than he could run.

Suddenly Bear cocked his head and held up his hand.

"Do you see that?" he whispered.

5

DEEP FREEZE

Joe squinted and looked. Bear pointed at a thick cluster of bushes at the bottom of the slope but Joe couldn't see anything unusual. It was just a scrappy bunch of bushes.

"There's something there," Bear said, frowning. "If it's what I think it is, we need to investigate."

Bear and Joe crept forward towards the bushes, but it was only when Bear parted some of the leaves, that Joe saw it for himself.

A reindeer was caught up by its massive antlers in a tangle of branches and stalks. It lay slumped on the ground.

"Is it...?" Joe couldn't say the word.

"Dead?" said Bear, leaning down and placing his hand on its neck. "Yes. But not long ago."

Joe stared. He realised that this was the closest to a wild animal he had ever been in real life.

"How did it die?" he asked.

Bear pointed to one of the reindeer's legs. It was bent in a weird way.

"It must have broken its leg and then got caught up in the bushes. It would have struggled for a bit.

But out here, breaking a leg is a death sentence for an animal like this. It probably died of exhaustion."

"So what do we do?" Joe said.

"Well, this will feed a lot of other animals round here. It hasn't frozen yet, so it's really fresh."

Bear cut the antlers free of the bushes. Then he and Joe dragged the reindeer out into the open.

"Now we need to gut and skin it, before it freezes solid," Bear said.

"Gut it?" Joe asked.

"I mean, take out the stomach and innards. They go off very quickly

and they could poison the rest of
the meat. Without them, the body
will freeze naturally and be safe
to eat for weeks."

Joe's jaw dropped as he realised
what Bear was going to do.

"You mean we're going to eat it?"

"We're going to take enough to
last us a day or two," Bear agreed.
He smiled softly. "I know, it can seem
harsh, but survivors can't afford to
be sentimental. Taking food that
becomes available saves us having
to spend time and effort to get it
later."

Bear cut a slit down the front of
the reindeer, and pulled its fur apart.

The reindeer's innards were like
stinky, rubbery bags all jostled
together. Bear pulled them out
onto the snow in a slopping,
quivering heap that steamed
gently in the freezing air.

"There's a small spade in my
rucksack," Bear said. "Please could
you dig a hole in the snow to bury
these in? And then we'll dig another
hole big enough to take the reindeer."

While Joe got to work digging, Bear
started to remove the reindeer's fur.

"This is something else we can use.
This guy's fur is perfect insulation.

It could keep him warm in a minus
fifty-degree winter, so it will do for
us too. But I have to remove it quickly.
Soon it'll be frozen and impossible to
work with."

Bear left the fur on the reindeer's
head, and its legs below the knees.
Everywhere else, he used the knife
and his fingers to separate skin
from the red flesh underneath.

After a few minutes the fur came
away completely, like a reindeer-
shaped rug.

Then Bear used the knife to cut
off one of the reindeer's rear legs.

"Fortunately we don't have to worry
about keeping this refrigerated."

"It will just freeze naturally,"
Joe realised.

"That's right! Now, let's get
our friend buried, somewhere the
predators can't get at him."

Between them, Joe and Bear
dragged the reindeer over to the hole
Joe had started and made it deeper.

"It's a shame we have to leave
so much," Joe said, as they covered
it up. "It seems like a waste."

"We can't take it," Bear agreed,
"but maybe others will. We're going
to mark this spot so that any other
explorers who come this way will
be able to find it — and so can we,
if we need to come back."

Joe looked around. The endless waste of snow and ice looked back. There was no sign of humans anywhere. Suddenly Joe felt very lonely. He was extremely glad he had Bear for company.

Bear cut a branch and jammed it into the ground.

"In a place like this," Bear said seriously, "you do what you can for your fellow explorers. Maybe we'll never know if we've helped someone today – but we will know we tried."

Bear tore a coloured scrap of cloth from his rucksack and tied it to the top of the branch, so that it fluttered like a little red flag.

"The best way to mark things in a place like this is with something that's obviously artificial. It stands out a mile."

Joe and Bear together folded up the fur. Bear opened up his rucksack.

"Okay ... not enough room in here for everything now. Not with the fur and the leg. Do you mind doing some carrying?"

"Sure, no problem. But I don't have a bag."

Bear grinned. "Leave that to me."

Bear pulled out a tarpaulin and rolled the leg up in it. There were metal eyelets in the tarpaulin at each corner. He folded the two ends together and tied them together, with a piece of string threaded through the eyelets.

Now the folded tarpaulin
was a continuous tube.

Bear looped it over Joe's arms
and head, and folded it back behind
his neck. Now the tarpaulin ran from
under one arm, up over one shoulder,
around Joe's neck and down under
the other arm.

Joe could feel the weight of the leg
pulling his shoulders back. It wasn't
anything he couldn't handle, and it
all felt nicely balanced.

They took a drink from the bottle.
Sure enough, the snow had melted
into cold, tasteless water.

Joe and Bear started to walk
again, and after a few hundred
metres, Joe looked back. He could
still see the fluttering red scrap.

It was the only splash of colour in the whole landscape. Anyone who looked that way would see it immediately.

Well, Joe thought, maybe the reindeer meat would help someone else one day.

Joe turned back to the way ahead, and his own problems.

There was still a lot of wilderness ahead to get lost in, he thought nervously. But, hey, maybe someone would have left *them* a marker too ...

6

PIECES OF THE JIGSAW

Joe and Bear trudged through a forest
of silvery trees. Joe wasn't really
sure what kind of tree they were, but
he checked and saw that there was
moss on some of them. Joe was still
determined to get this navigation
thing right.

He thought hard for a moment.

If he and Bear were going *east*,
and moss was on the *north* side,
then the moss should be on the
left. Or was it the right?

The first tree Joe looked at, he
thought the moss *might* be on the
north side. It was on Joe's left, which
was where north would be if they
really were going east.

Next to it was a tree with the moss
spread all over the trunk. Then there
was a tree with no moss at all. The
trees couldn't agree!

Joe must have made a frustrated
noise. Bear smiled at him.

"Are you okay, buddy?"

Joe gritted his teeth and explained. Bear nodded, understanding.

"Well, it's like the prevailing wind. Moss is *mostly* on the north side, but it isn't always one hundred per cent like that. Here's another one you can try."

A tree had toppled over. Bear pointed at the rings inside the trunk. They started in the middle and then grew larger as you got nearer the outside of the tree.

"A tree gets a new ring each year it's alive, during the growth season. But can you see here – the rings are slightly thicker on this side? That's because this side got more sun. So, that way is south. Of course, you need to find a fallen tree to see that one."

Bear stood up and held up his hands, with his fingers spread.

"So, you see, you can have lots of little clues. Moss. Rings. Wind. Plants. Sastrugi. They're all pieces in a jigsaw."

Then Bear clasped his hands so that his fingers were all linked.

"If you put them all together, Nature gives you the big picture, and *that's* the one to look at."

Soon after that, they were walking along a bank where the snow had piled up. Bear sunk his stick into the snow by a good metre, and looked pleased.

"This is just what we need for our midday break."

"What, snow?" Joe asked in surprise. "Won't it be cold?"

Bear smiled. "You'll see!"

They used their gloved hands like spades to dig out a trench in the powdery snow.

Soon they had a hole in the side
of the bank that was about a metre
deep, and wide enough for them
to sit side by side.

Bear scooped out one last little
trench in the floor.

"This is a gutter for the cold air
to sink into. Now, you look around
for some branches we can put over
this, and I'll make a fire."

Joe made sure he stayed within
sight of Bear as he walked off into
the woods. Eventually, he found
a couple of fallen branches. They
were about his size and they still
had leaves on them. Joe dragged
them back to the trench.

Bear had lined the trench with the reindeer fur, and built a fire in front. He and Joe laid the branches over the top of the hole.

Bear and Joe sat inside the hole on the reindeer fur, covered over by the branches as a roof. The fire crackled. To Joe's surprise, he actually felt warm.

"So, we've got fur underneath us," Joe worked out, "and a roof to keep the warm air in."

Bear had made a small pile of fragments of the silvery tree bark next to the fire. He leaned forward and added another piece to the flames.

"And we've got a fire," Bear agreed with a smile. "Birch bark is full of flammable sap, so it's perfect for the job."

So, now Joe knew what the trees were called.

Bear shaved some bits of meat off the frozen reindeer leg, and held them on a piece of wood over the flames to sizzle. They smelled, and tasted, delicious.

They washed the meat down with more meltwater, and Joe filled the bottle up again with snow.

When they stood up again Joe got a chance to test his navigation skills.

"So, which way should we head now?" Bear asked, as he packed up the reindeer fur.

Joe finished kicking snow over the fire to put it out, and looked around. He pointed.

"That way?"

"Spot on!" Bear smiled. "What told you?"

"I just saw our footprints from where we walked up, and kept going in that direction," Joe said shyly.

Bear laughed.

"Well, that's another piece of the jigsaw! The obvious markers are the best, but you can still look for other clues if there aren't any. Like, do you notice that the tree branches on the west side are covered with snow, but not on the east?"

"Because the wind blows from west to east," Joe worked out, "so that's where the snow sticks."

"You've got it. You're really picking this up well, Joe."

Joe felt good for working out
their direction from the footprints.
And he felt even better for Bear's
encouragement.

After walking a few more minutes,
they came to a frozen-over stream.
The ice was thin enough to see the
water moving underneath.

"We might have to cross this," said
Bear, "but for the moment it's going
in pretty much the right direction, so
let's see what happens if we follow
it."

Pretty much the right direction? Joe
felt an immediate stab of anxiety.

He could see with his own eyes
that the stream wound back and

forth between the trees. If they followed the stream then they wouldn't be heading due east any more!

He tried to make himself calm down.

Okay, they were changing direction. But there would still be other clues.

They walked for a few minutes more, until the trees ran out. There were a few metres of clear ground, and then the stream ran right over a cliff.

The cliff didn't look high, Joe thought. Four or five metres. Still a bit too far to jump.

He started to walk forward, to see exactly how high the cliff was. Bear put a hand on his shoulder.

"Careful. We can't get too close. Do you see the way the snow is piled up along the edge? I'll bet you it's overhanging the rock-face. It will collapse if we stand on it – and it could fall on us if we tried to climb down."

Joe felt his spirits plummet. He looked back at their footprints, the way they had come.

"So ... do we have to find another way?"

7

SUNNY SIDE UP

The one place the snow didn't overhang was the waterfall itself. Bear carefully followed the frozen stream to the edge and peered down. Then he smiled back at Joe.

"This is our way down."

He stepped back, and took a rope and a small axe from his rucksack.

Joe couldn't see anything they could fix the rope to. The trees were too far away.

Bear took the axe and bashed a hole into the ice itself. Then he bashed another, about a metre further on.

Bear doubled the rope up into two parallel strands, and pushed the loop that joined them in through the top hole. He fished it out of the bottom one and kept pulling, until the two doubled-up pieces on either side of the holes were about the same length.

Now he had four strands of rope in his hand, side by side – two going into one hole, two coming out of the other.

Joe started to understand.

"Now it's doubled up," he said,
"so you just have to pull on one end
and it will all come down after us."

Bear nodded.

"A rope's far too valuable to just
abandon. And if we did it with just one
length then our weight might make
it cut through the ice so it won't hold
us – but two strands should pad it
out. I need to go first, to double-
check that it's safe. Will you be
okay coming down after me?"

Joe smiled.

"I get confused about left and right,
but I think I can do straight down!"

Bear laughed.

"Brilliant! Let's go, then."

First, they threw Bear's rucksack and Joe's reindeer leg sling down the cliff ahead of them.

"It makes us both slightly lighter, and nothing's going to break," Bear said.

He took the four strands of rope in his hands and walked backwards over the fall.

"There are rocks sticking out through the ice," he called up, "so double-check there are plenty of footholds for you. Just never let go of the rope with one hand until you're holding it firm with the other. And only move one foot at a time."

A couple of minutes later, it was Joe's turn.

Joe let himself down, step by step, foothold to foothold. The ice creaked and groaned.

Joe could hear the water trickling, and see it, a few centimetres in front of him, through the ice.

The rope strands were taut with the strain of his weight. It was a relief when his feet finally touched the ground.

Bear pulled on one end of the doubled-up rope. The other end shot upwards. A few seconds later, the whole rope dropped down at their feet. Bear coiled it up so that it could go back in his rucksack.

While he did that, Joe looked around. He fought back a stab of worry. Did the stream still go the same direction as up above? He wasn't sure it did.

So, how would they know which way to head?

Joe suddenly realised he had one massive clue to the direction they should take, right at his feet.

"We're heading for a lake, right?" he said. "And this stream must go somewhere ..."

Bear smiled, and nodded.

"You're right, Joe. This stream almost certainly goes into the lake. All the watercourses around here will end up in it."

"So if we follow it, we'll get there!" Joe said happily.

It didn't matter that the stream twisted and turned. If they followed it then they were absolutely guaranteed to get wherever it was going.

Soon the stream was flowing through a valley that wound and wiggled along. The valley sides were covered with bushes and small trees that stuck up out of the snow. Their stalks and twigs were dark and bare.

Joe noticed one side of the valley was darker than the other, because there were more bushes there. He bounced a few explanations around in his head. He could think of one straight away.

"Is this the side that faces south?"

he asked eventually. Joe pointed
at the side with more bushes.

Bear nodded, with a smile.

"That's right, buddy. And the tree
branches are longer, too. It's the side
that gets more sun, so the plants
get more energy. Did you spot that?
You're turning into such a great
navigator!"

Joe spent the rest of the trek
gazing around him, trying to take
in more clues.

He was the one moving. *Nature*
stayed still. The clues didn't shift
around when he wasn't looking.
He could trust the world to stay
where it was.

He could do this!

Just as Joe was feeling confident,
the valley ran out. The trees stopped,
and the smooth surface of the
frozen stream ran into a much
wider, smoother surface of ice.

The lake!

Ice stretched away in every
direction. There had to be a mile
of it or more, before it reached
the trees on the other side.

Joe smiled to himself. They had walked for hours – most of the day – and the sky was turning red as the sun set. He'd learned to navigate and now they were right where Bear had expected them to be.

But the good feeling only lasted a second. Hadn't Bear said they were heading for a hunting lodge?

Joe looked around.

There was no sign of any kind of building. Just trees, and snow, and more trees, and more snow. All that careful navigating, Joe moaned to himself, and they'd still reached the wrong bit?

"This *is* the lake, isn't it?" he asked, just to be sure.

Bear nodded.

"We're absolutely where we want to be, Joe," he said. "Come over here."

Joe trudged after Bear and tried to feel as cheerful as Bear sounded. Okay, it was the right lake. But where was the lodge, then?

That was when he noticed that a pile of snow by the trees had a metal chimney sticking out of it.

8

ICE AND FIRE

The chimney was the only clue.
The rest of the lodge was just
a smooth mound of snow.

"The door probably faces the
lake," Bear said, "so we'll dig it
out on this side."

He and Joe dug into the snow,
like when they had made the midday

trench, scooping out large chunks
until they were both covered with
white powder. A wooden wall slowly
appeared, with a door, and a window
of dirty, cloudy plastic.

"We'll leave the rest of the snow
for insulation," Bear said, and pushed
the door open. The inside was just as
cold as out, but at least it was snow-
free.

The lodge was one big room. In the
dim light, Joe saw a table and some
shelves, with bits and pieces on them.
There was a metal stove, a pile of
sticks and logs and a couple of bunks.

Bear went straight to the stove.
On the shelves next to it there was a
box of matches, and an old newspaper

left by a previous explorer. The pages were yellow with age, and bone dry. Bear passed it to Joe.

"Joe, please could you tear up about a quarter of the pages? We don't want to waste the whole thing. Crumple them up into little balls."

While Joe did that, Bear grabbed a couple of armfuls of wood and built up a pile inside the stove. First, the paper that Joe had crumpled, then smaller bits of wood on top of it, then a couple of logs on top of that.

Once it was all in, he set fire to the paper with the box of matches. Yellow flame was spreading through the paper as Bear shut the metal door.

"We'll keep it fed while we're here, and we'll soon be warm and toasty!" he said. "And we can cook us some more reindeer, too."

They drank melted snow, and fried some strips of reindeer meat in a metal pan on top of the stove. It tasted even better than their lunch. By now, the lodge felt as warm as Joe's tent back at Camp. They left the rest of the leg outside, in nature's freezer.

"Reindeer's fine," Bear said, as they washed it down with more pine-needle tea, "but we could do with some fish for breakfast."

"Tasty!" Joe agreed.

"So, we're going to need some things. There's a ball of string in the rucksack, if you can bring that. We'll be building another fire out on the ice, so we'll take these bits of kindling and wood here, and replace them for other explorers before we leave tomorrow."

"Will the ice hold our weight?" Joe asked as they went outside. "The ice on the stream looked quite thin."

Joe had tried to stand on a frozen fish pond back home. He had gone straight through and got soaked. Out here, the result would be a lot worse.

Bear smiled as he walked onto the ice and stamped his foot.

"The stream was moving, so it didn't freeze. Still water, in this temperature, will be fine. It needs to be at least five centimetres thick to hold your weight, but this will be more than that."

Bear stamped again. "If you're ever unsure, a good way is to give it a hard prod with your stick, three times. If it doesn't go through after that, it'll be okay."

Bear and Joe went out onto the ice for about fifty metres, with their arms full of sticks and logs and bits of birch bark. Joe went back to get a second load of wood – a pile of spruce branches which Bear had pointed out – while Bear started to cut a hole in the ice.

By the time Joe got back, Bear had used the axe and his knife to cut a hole in the ice as wide as a football. As Bear had promised, the ice was thick – Joe guessed ten centimetres or more – and the water was dark.

"Could you pass me some string, please?" Bear said.

He cut off a length about a metre long. Then he snapped a small twig off one of their bits of wood, about half the length of Joe's little finger. With his knife, he cut away the bark and sharpened the two ends to points.

"Hold this, please?"

Joe held the bit of wood while
Bear tied the end of the string
around its middle.

"This is called a gorge hook,"
Bear said.

Bear took the wood and the string,
and held them so they were parallel.
Then he pushed the pointed wood
into a bit of reindeer meat so that
one end came out of the other side.

"The fish comes along for a nibble, and gets the bait. But the bait is holding the hook parallel to the string. Without the bait, the hook swings around and catches in the fish's mouth, so it can't get free," Bear explained. "Now, the last thing we do is build a fire."

Bear and Joe made a pile of the sticks and bits of wood they had brought, next to the hole. It started with lots of thin twigs and fragments of wood. On top, Bear put all the bits of birch bark.

"While I get this going, could you gather up those spruce branches into a bundle?" Bear said. "We want all the leafy ends packed together. You'll see why."

Joe collected as much wood as he could while Bear set the fire alight.

The flame took over the pile as the oils in the bark caught fire, crackling its way through the twigs and licking up against the bark bits. Soon, orange flame rose cheerfully up into the sky.

Joe thought that maybe the fire was for them, to keep them warm while they waited for a fish to bite. But that seemed a lot of effort to go to, when they could just wait in their nice, warm lodge. He tried to think of non-obvious reasons, and got one.

"I suppose this attracts them?" he said.

Joe imagined the glow of the flame from a fish's point of view, through the ice.

Bear nodded.

"It's the brightest thing around, including underwater. They'll come to investigate, and find a nice bit of reindeer meat waiting for them."

Bear tied the string onto a stick, which he laid across the hole. The hook and bait disappeared into the water.

"And now the spruce branches ..." he said.

They packed the leafy ends of the branches into the hole around the fishing line. The branches pressed against each other, and against the side of the hole, so they stayed in place.

"And that stops the hole freezing over," Bear said. "You wouldn't believe how many ice-fishing trips have been wasted because people forgot to do that!"

Bear looked at Joe seriously. "Now, fish won't be the only creatures attracted to the fire. There are bears and wolves out here – so we should get back indoors. A night in the warm, and tomorrow we should reach the coast!"

9

ONE LITTLE FISHY

Daylight crept in through the grimy window. Joe stirred and stretched himself awake beneath the warm woollen blankets.

In the other bunk across the room, Bear was still asleep.

Joe's stomach growled. It reminded him of their plans for breakfast.

Had they caught a fish? It would be cool to go and see.

He pulled his outdoor gear back on, and laced up his boots. There was a pencil stub on the table. Joe scrawled a quick note on one of the bits of paper: 'going to check fish'.

Bear had said they were a team, and leaving a note felt like something a team member would do.

Joe was also thirsty. There was an old metal water bottle with a leather strap on the shelf by the door, left by some other user of the lodge.

Joe decided to fill the bottle up with snow to melt. He slung it over

his shoulder, pulled his hood up,
and stepped outside.

He had forgotten exactly how cold
it was outside until he felt it bite into
his exposed face. He gasped, and the
air went into his lungs too. Man, that
was cold!

Joe was glad he still had warm air
inside his clothes and against his skin.
He was well wrapped up in good Arctic
clothing, and protected from the wind.

First things first. Joe scooped
snow into the water bottle, and
stuck it inside his coat, quickly,
so as not to let the warmth out.

Then he walked down to the
edge of the lake.

That bit was easy. All he had to
do was follow yesterday's footprints.
Snow had drifted during the night and
the footprints were faint, but they
were still visible.

Then Joe looked out over the lake.

He couldn't see the other side.
In fact, it was hard to tell how far
he could see. A white mist hung
over the ice. There was nothing
firm to look at.

Joe stood and stared. He couldn't
see any footprints, or the fishing hole.
Not even the fire next to it. Joe knew

it would have burnt out long ago,
but there should still be a pile of
burnt wood and ashes.

All he could see was white,
directionless mist. If Joe wanted
fish for breakfast, he'd have to
go into the mist.

Joe almost turned back. But
then he looked down at the ice.

Sastrugi!

He hadn't thought to look for them
the night before. He had just walked
with Bear in a straight line onto the
ice, with his arms full of wood.

This morning, he noticed that the wind-blown patterns ran diagonally across the ice.

Now Joe knew he could do this. He had his direction, from their footprints on land. If he kept the sastrugi like that, diagonal, then he would be going in a straight line.

Joe started walking.

The white mist slowly grew thick around him. Very soon, Joe couldn't see anything ahead – or behind him, either. The land and the trees had vanished into the white blur.

But he could see the sastrugi.

"Just keep walking," he muttered.

"Just keep walking..."

Joe kept the sastrugi diagonal,
and kept going.

A grey spot appeared in the mist.
Dead ahead. Joe's heart started to
beat faster.

And then he was standing by a pile
of ashes, next to a hole in the ice
stuffed with spruce branches. The
fire had melted a small dip in the
ice, but the ice was too thick for
it to go all the way through.

"Yes!" Joe punched the air.

The spruce branches had kept the
hole open during the freezing night.
Joe pushed them apart to get at the

fishing stick with the line attached to it. The line vanished into the water.

Joe tugged it between thumb and forefinger. It felt like there was a weight on the other end. Joe felt the excitement growing inside him. He gave the line another tug.

There was a sudden yank on the other end and the line was pulled out of his fingers. Only the fact that it was tied to the stick stopped it from disappearing into the water.

"We've caught a fish! Go us!" Joe exclaimed.

He gave the line another tug, and this time he held onto it. He could feel the fish pulling against it, straining ...

Suddenly, he realised what might happen. If he just kept yanking on the line, the fish would keep fighting back and the line would snap. The fish would get away and all that work would have been for nothing.

Joe gently let the line back into
the water. That was close. Okay,
so he didn't know what to do next.
But Bear would. Now Joe just had
to go and get him.

Joe knew that all he had to do was
turn round and follow his footprints...

Or did he?

When he'd got to the hole he'd
walked around it. The ground was
a blur of footprints. And the white
mist worked both ways. You couldn't
see where you were going – or where
you had come from, either.

If he got this wrong, then he could
spend the rest of his life walking round
and round in circles on the lake ...

"Calm down, Joe," he muttered to himself. Whichever direction he went, he would come to land eventually. It wasn't going to move.

And he still had the sastrugi. They had guided him here, they could guide him back.

Joe made himself remember how the fire and the hole had been when he first saw them. He walked around, without taking his eyes off them, until they were in the same places again.

Fire *there*. Hole *there*. Sastrugi going *that* way.

So, he must have his back to the way he had come. Joe turned around on the spot, exactly half a circle. He made a note of which way the sastrugi were going now, and started walking.

A minute later, Joe was grinning from ear to ear. When he came out of the mist he was bang on target. Joe followed his own footprints back up to the lodge, with a song in his heart.

Joe put his hand on the door to go in. Then he paused and took one last, satisfied look back. Everything was exactly where it should be, and that included him.

He turned back to the lodge and stepped in.

"Hey, Bear, we got a fish!" he called.

Joe stopped, blinking in surprise.
Where was Bear?

In fact, where was the lodge?

The snow?

The lake?

Joe was standing on ground covered
with dead leaves and pine needles.
He was in his jeans and T-shirt and
trainers.

And he was warm.

10

A LOT OF BOTTLE

Joe was back at Camp – but just as
lost as he had been when he left.

He turned in a slow circle and
looked at the trees.

He could see the moss, and the
way the trees grew. He could make
a stab at which way was south. But
that didn't help if he didn't know

which direction the meal tent was in, did it?

"C'mon," he said quietly. "You can do this. Bear showed you how."

Part of him wanted to doubt it all. Joe knew he couldn't have got to the Arctic and back, just like that. He remembered how dizzy he had felt. It must be something to do with that. Something weird inside his head.

But he clearly remembered Bear telling him to look for clues. Maybe it was worth a try.

Joe thought back to his lunch with his friends. He closed his eyes and pictured it.

They had chosen a table in the shade. It had been in a tree's shadow. So, the tree had been between the sun and the table.

He had walked away from the table, in the same direction as the shadow.

So, he had walked away from the sun.

Which meant that now Joe just had to walk *towards* the sun, and he would be back where he started!

Joe's heart pounded with excitement as he started to follow the shadows back through the trees. He was trusting himself to a dream. But somehow he felt confident. Even if he had dreamed it, it made sense.

Soon his ears told him he was
on the right track. He could hear
the sounds of kids having lunch,
and he felt even more confident.

A couple of minutes later, he
was back in the clearing. And
there were his friends.

Even better, there was his lunch.
No one had eaten it. Result! Joe felt
extra hungry. He remembered how
he'd walked all day and not even
eaten the fish for breakfast.

Joe smiled and shook his head.
Not real! he reminded himself. But
even if it had just been a weird kind
of daydream, his body seemed to
think it had been real.

"Hi, guys." Joe sat down. Something was bumping against his hip so he pushed it aside. "Thanks for leaving my lunch."

"We were only half sure you weren't coming back," said Omar.

"So we only ate half your food," Lily said with a smile. Joe laughed.

"Cheers, everyone!"

But he didn't have very long to finish it. One of the leaders came along, clapping her hands.

"Okay, time for afternoon activities! And remember that two o'clock is the deadline for tomorrow's sign-up, so that gives you about ten minutes if

you haven't already. No sign-up,
no activity."

Joe ate quickly and got up to go.
He still needed to put his name
down for tomorrow.

Mia still had about half her
lunch left and was chatting to Lily,
seemingly unaware of the time.

"Hey, Mia, what are you doing
tomorrow?" Lily asked.

"I haven't signed up yet. But it
doesn't matter."

"You'd better hurry up then!
You've got ... eight minutes."

"Oh, it'll be fine, don't worry about it.

I'll just decide tomorrow, they'll sort it out for me."

"But if you don't sign up for something..."

"Look, Lily, it's just a stupid rule. It doesn't really matter, okay?"

Mia was starting to sound annoyed. She never liked being told what to do, even when the rules were there for her benefit. She just wanted to do her own thing, even when it caused problems for other people. Somehow Mia just couldn't ever seem to admit that she was in the wrong.

Joe supposed he had been a bit the same with directions. People had tried to help him, but he'd just ignored them. He'd had a mental block about it. But then the adventure in the Arctic with Bear had totally sorted his head out.

"Is that in case you get thirsty?" Omar asked as Joe caught up.

Joe looked down.

Hanging by a leather strap across his shoulder was a metal water bottle.

The water bottle Joe had taken from the lodge in the snow, next to a frozen lake.

If this bottle was real then his Arctic adventure had been real too!

Joe looked back. Mia was still picking through her food.

"Uh, Omar – put my name down for tomorrow for whatever you're doing, would you? I just forgot something..."

"Okay, will do. See you in a bit."

Joe started walking back towards Mia. He wasn't sure what he would say when he got there but he knew he had something important to tell her. Something that might lead her to Bear.

The water bottle bumped against his hip again – and against something in his pocket. The compass! Joe took it out and looked at it.

It just had the usual four directions. Somehow, though, Joe was certain that the compass was the answer.

Mia looked up at Joe cheerfully.

"Hi, Joe. Forget something?"

"Uh. No."

Joe realised that she might think he was really weird. But it was a risk worth taking. He put the compass down on the table.

"I just thought you might like this. You know. Consider it a gift."

The End

Bear Grylls got the taste for adventure at a young age from his father, a former Royal Marine. After school, Bear joined the Reserve SAS, then went on to become one of the youngest ever people to climb Mount Everest, just two years after breaking his back in three places during a parachute jump.

Amongst other adventures he has led expeditions to the Arctic and the Antarctic, crossed oceans and set world records in skydiving and paragliding.

Bear is also a bestselling author and the host of television programmes such as *Survival School* and *The Island*.

He has shared his survival skills with people all over the world, and has taken many famous movie stars and sports stars on adventures – and even President Barack Obama!

Bear Grylls is Chief Scout to the UK Scouting Association, encouraging young people to

have great adventures, follow
their dreams and to look after
their friends. Bear is also honorary
Colonel to the Royal Marine
Commandos.

When Bear's not travelling the
world, he lives with his wife and
three sons on a barge in London,
or on an island off the coast of
Wales.

Find out more at
www.beargrylls.com

This brilliant **Bear Grylls Adventure** is set in a reader-friendly font and design, for maximum enjoyment for everyone.

The font we have used is called OpenDyslexic. You can find out more about it here: **www.opendyslexic.org**

Dyslexia affects as many as 1 in 10 people, and often makes reading more difficult. We wanted to make our books as easy to enjoy as possible, so this special font and a design with lots of space helps us do just that.

Not everyone with difficulty reading has dyslexia, and not everyone with dyslexia has the same difficulties. You can find out more about dyslexia on these wonderful websites:

The Dyslexia Association: **dyslexia.uk.net**

British Dyslexia Association: **bdadyslexia.org.uk**

Dyslexia Scotland: **www.dyslexiascotland.org.uk**

DID YOU KNOW?

• The Arctic Circle is the northernmost part of Planet Earth – its name comes from the Greek word Arktos, meaning 'near the bear'. The constellations of stars in the northern sky, Ursa Major (Great Bear) and Ursa Minor (Little Bear) can be seen very clearly in the Arctic.

• The Arctic tundra is a vast, treeless plain which is covered with permafrost – that means that the ground is frozen so that roots cannot penetrate the soil. In winter the ground is covered with snow, and in summer the top layer melts enough that flowers, grasses, moss and lichen can grow. It can be colder than -50°C in winter.

- There are two North Poles! The Geographic North Pole is the direction of true north, where latitude and longitude lines meet. The Magnetic North Pole is the point where all the planet's magnetic fields point downwards – so compass needles will point south. The Magnetic North Pole moves location. No one knows which one Father Christmas lives at . . .

- The Geographic North Pole is located in the middle of the Arctic Ocean in waters that are permanently covered with shifting ice. Many explorers have attempted to reach it, but the harsh conditions mean that often these expeditions have had tragic endings. Lots of people have claimed to reach the North Pole, but scientists say the first expedition that can be independently proved was by Roald Amundsen on 12th May 1926, who travelled in an airship.

•Reindeer are just some of the amazing animals that live in the freezing temperatures of the Arctic. Reindeer travel long distances and live in massive herds — the largest in the world has over 500,000 reindeer! Beware of their antlers — both male and female reindeer grow antlers and use them to defend the food they've found. So don't get between Rudolph and his dinner!

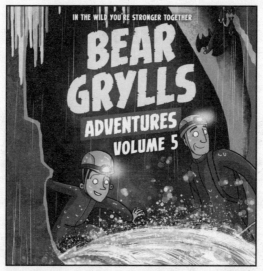

Cave Challenge & Mountain Challenge

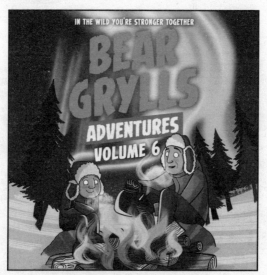

Arctic Challenge & Sailing Challenge

Available at all audiobook retailers

THE BEAR GRYLLS

ADVENTURES SERIES

FOR MORE INFORMATION ON
BEAR GRYLLS, CHECK OUT

beargrylls.com